THE
LITTLEST LLAMA

BY **Jane Buxton**

ILLUSTRATED BY **Jenny Cooper**

STERLING

New York / London

This one is for William, my son, friend, and critic, with love —J. B.
For Jane, and all her family of llamas —J. C.

As you read this book, can you find . . .
a rattlesnake?
some chinchillas?
a cougar?
an Andean condor?
a few nine-banded armadillos?
some guinea pigs?

GLOSSARY:

altiplano—a high plain, such as is found in the Andes Mountains of South America

spit—llamas sometimes spit at one another when they are annoyed or angry

hum—humming is one way llamas communicate

mañana—the Spanish word for "tomorrow"

STERLING and the distinctive Sterling logo are registered trademarks of Sterling Publishing Co., Inc.

Library of Congress Cataloging-in-Publication Data Available

10 9 8 7 6 5 4 3 2 1

Published by Sterling Publishing Co., Inc. 387 Park Avenue South, New York, NY 10016
Text copyright © 2008 by Jane Buxton ✦ Illustrations copyright © 2008 by Jenny Cooper
Distributed in Canada by Sterling Publishing c/o Canadian Manda Group, 165 Dufferin Street, Toronto, Ontario, Canada M6K 3H6.
Distributed in the United Kingdom by GMC Distribution Services, Castle Place, 166 High Street, Lewes, East Sussex, England BN7 1XU.
Distributed in Australia by Capricorn Link (Australia) Pty. Ltd., P.O. Box 704, Windsor, NSW 2756, Australia.
Printed in China. All rights reserved

Sterling ISBN-13: 978-1-4027-5277-3
ISBN-10: 1-4027-5277-6

For information about custom editions, special sales, premium and corporate purchases, please contact
Sterling Special Sales Department at 800-805-5489 or specialsales@sterlingpublishing.com.

On the high *altiplano,* out under the sun,
lived lots of big llamas—and one little one.

The littlest llama just wanted to play,
neck-wrestling, jumping, and chasing all day.

But the grown-up llamas had work to do.
They had food to find and cud to chew.

They had fights to sort out. They had itches to scratch.
They had dust baths to take in the dust-bathing patch.

They had water to search for and look-out to keep
for snakes that slither and lions that creep.

There was no one to play with the littlest llama.
No one had time, not even his mama.

"I'm having a bath in the dust patch," she said.
"Go off and play with your sisters instead."

So he ran to his sisters, both browsing the trees.
"Play with me! Play with me! Play with me, please!"

"No!" spat his sisters. "We don't want to play.
We don't want to neck-wrestle. Please go away."

So the littlest llama skipped, hopped, and ran.
He dashed through the bushes and found his old gran.

"Littlest llama, you're being a pest,"
 said his grumpy old granny. "Just leave me to rest.

I don't want to play. I just want to sit.
Stop that at once, or I'm going to spit!"

So the littlest llama went racing away,
looking for someone who might want to play.

Down past the bushes he heard a low groan,
and he found his fat auntie there, all on her own.

She said, "Little llama, please go away.
I'm doing something important today."

The littlest llama, now four times rejected,
was feeling unwanted and sad and dejected.

Without even saying good-bye to his mama,
away from his herd walked the littlest llama.

He wanted a playmate. He wanted a friend.
Maybe he'd find someone just round the bend.

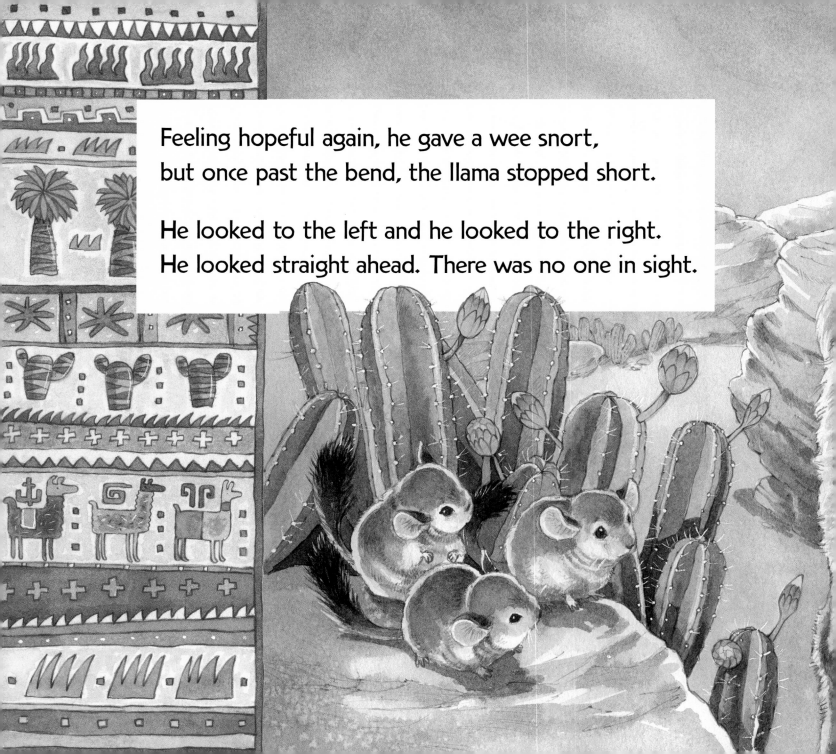

Feeling hopeful again, he gave a wee snort,
but once past the bend, the llama stopped short.

He looked to the left and he looked to the right.
He looked straight ahead. There was no one in sight.

Onward he went, down a long stony ridge,
till he came to a gorge with a rickety bridge.

Crossing the bridge he felt wonderfully brave.
He walked past some rocks and he walked past a cave.

He walked on and on in the hot noonday sun.
He was looking for friends. He was looking for fun.

But no friends could he find, our littlest llama.
He was tired. He was hungry. And he missed his mama.

Then—fierce and orange and round like the sun—
a monster bounced after him. Run, llama, run!

As he hurtled for home he was not feeling brave.
He fled past the houses and raced past the cave.

When he came to the rocks, he slowed to a trot.
His legs were so tired and the sun blazing hot.

He turned and looked back and was thankful to find
that the horrible monster was left far behind.

He clattered back over the rickety bridge,
and wearily walked up the long stony ridge.

Back round the bend trudged the littlest llama,
and there were his sisters, his gran, and his mama.

And his auntie so slim and as proud as a queen,
with the littlest llama that he'd ever seen!

She was just newly born, and her coat was still wet.
Her legs were all wobbly. She couldn't walk yet.

She looked at our llama and staggered his way,
and hummed in her small baby voice, "Want to play?"

But the tired little llama lay down by his mama.
He smiled at his cousin and whispered, "*Mañana.*"